SASSY GRACIE

For Caroline *J.S.*

For my parents *P.P.*

First published 1998 by Macmillan Children's Books
a division of Macmillan Publishers Limited
25 Eccleston Place, London SW1W 9NF
and Basingstoke
Associated companies worldwide

ISBN 0 333 68427 3 (hardback)
ISBN 0 333 68428 1 (paperback)

Text copyright © 1998 James Sage
Illustrations copyright © 1998 Pierre Pratt

1 3 5 7 9 8 6 4 2

A CIP catalogue record for this book is available from the British Library.
Printed in Belgium by Proost International Book Production.

SASSY GRACIE

by James Sage
illustrated by Pierre Pratt

MACMILLAN CHILDREN'S BOOKS

Sassy Gracie had a pair of Big Red Shoes
with Big Red Heels that she loved to pieces.

Kiss, kiss! Kiss, kiss!

When she went prancing about in them . . .
which Cook said was far too often . . .
they sounded like this:
clunkety-CLUNK, clunkety-CLUNK!

Stop that dancing, Sassy Gracie!
It's getting on my nerves!

Now one day, which happened to be Cook's day off,
the Master of the big house came down to see her.
He walked with a big stick, which sounded like this:
Bumpety-BUMP! Bumpety-BUMP! Bumpety-BUMP!

*Sassy Gracie, I'm expecting a very important guest
for dinner. Two roast chickens will do nicely.*

So Sassy Gracie hurried off to market,
clunkety-CLUNK, clunkety-CLUNK!
where she bought two of the plumpest
little chickens she could find.

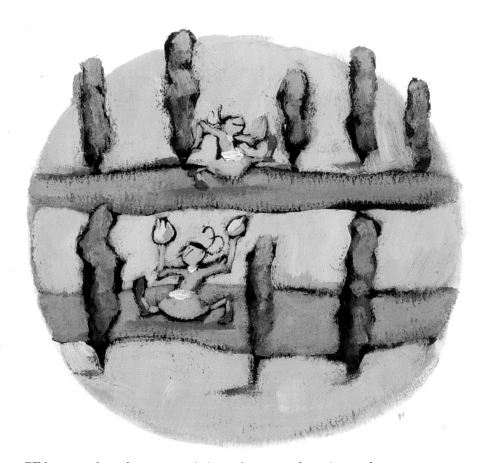

Then she hurried back to the big house.

Well, there wasn't much to do while the chickens
were roasting, except kick her heels by the stove.
And the more Sassy Gracie kicked her big red heels
the more she felt like dancing.

Cook not being here to stop me, you know!

So she did. She danced all round the kitchen,
clunkety-CLUNK . . .

. . . down the hall, clunkety-CLUNK,
around the best sitting room, clunkety-CLUNK,
through the dining room, clunkety-CLUNK,
in and out of the Master's library . . .

. . . and back to the kitchen.

Whew! Dancing sure can take it out of you!

Now, by this time, the chickens had cooked to a lovely golden brown, but the guest had still not appeared.

Sassy Gracie went to see her Master.

If that guest of yours doesn't show up soon, my chickens will be ruined!

So her Master sent the stable boy to look for the guest
and Sassy Gracie went clunkety-CLUNK, back to
her kitchen and took the chickens out of the oven.
As the chickens sat there cooling, Sassy Gracie began
to wonder if they really were cooked through or what.
So she thought she'd best have a little nibble of one.

Well, the wing's OK,
but that drumstick looks a bit iffy.

So she had another little nibble,

Just to make sure!

And another . . .

and another . . .

until the chicken was no more than
a spiky carcass of well-picked bones!

Eating all that chicken made her feel so frisky
that she started dancing all over again . . .

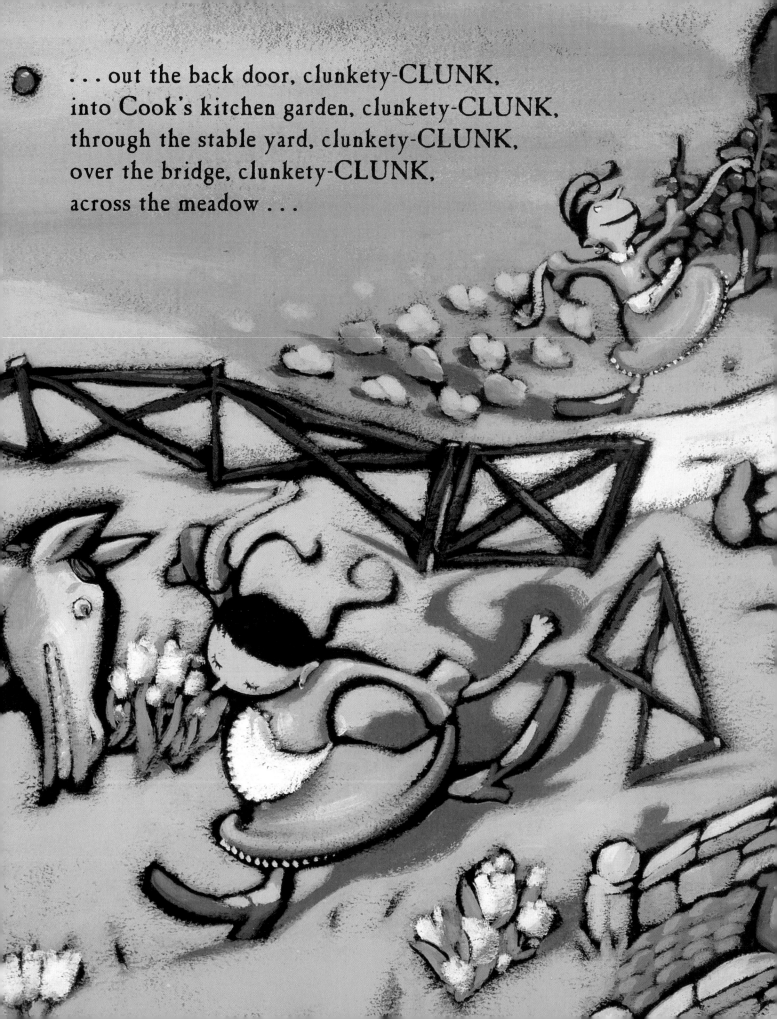

. . . out the back door, clunkety-CLUNK,
into Cook's kitchen garden, clunkety-CLUNK,
through the stable yard, clunkety-CLUNK,
over the bridge, clunkety-CLUNK,
across the meadow . . .

. . . and back to the kitchen, where she noticed
the second chicken still cooling on the table.
And she began to wonder if it could possibly
be as well cooked as the first.

Well, there is only one way to find out,
and that's to taste it. After all, the cook is
allowed a little nibble every now and then!

Which was more now than then . . .
for soon the second chicken was no more
than a spiky carcass of well-picked bones,
just like the first!

My oh my! that sure was tasty,
if I do say so myself.

And then she heard the Master call.

Sassy Gracie! Sassy Gracie!
My guest is arriving!
Get the dinner ready!

Oh dear! What was Sassy Gracie going to do now?
She had eaten both chickens!

Well, this is what she did. She scooted out the
back door and around the house to the front,
clunkety-CLUNK, clunkety-CLUNK,
where she bumped into the guest coming up the walk.

Crikey, Mister, are you in trouble! Puff, puff.
If I were you, I'd hot foot it home while the
going is good. Puff, puff. Because you're so
late, my Master is planning to give you two
big bumps on the head with his walking stick!
Puff, puff. Listen! You can hear him coming now.

And the guest listened.

And, sure enough, this is what he heard:

Bumpety-BUMP!

Bumpety-BUMP!

Bumpety-BUMP!

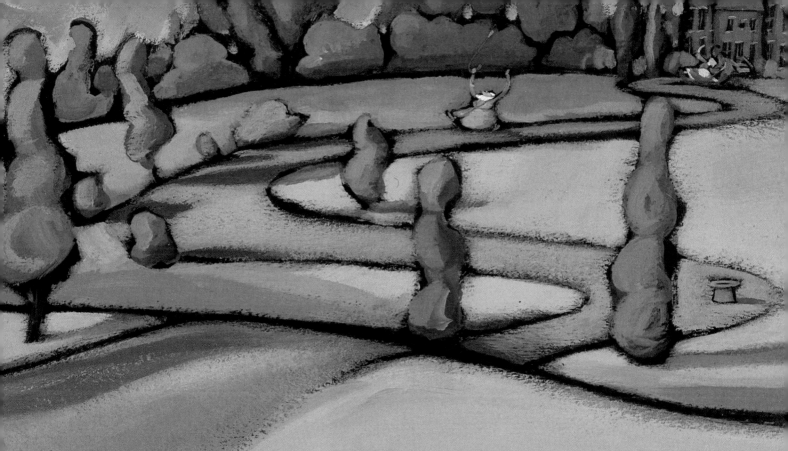

So naturally, he made tracks . . .
while Sassy Gracie scooted back into
the house, clunkety-CLUNK,
to speak to her Master.

That's a fine guest you invited!
He's run off with my two roast chickens!

Her Master was very annoyed.

You don't say! Both roast chickens? A fine guest, indeed!
He might at least have left me one to eat!

And away he ran, waving his walking stick in the air
and shouting:

Stop! Only one! All I want is one!

But the poor guest, thinking his host now meant to give him
one big bump on the head instead of two, ran all the faster.

And Sassy Gracie? Well,
she went prancing up the stairs,
clunkety-CLUNK, to her little
room at the top of the big house,
clunkety-CLUNK, and plopped
herself on her big brass bed,
CLUNK! where she kicked off
one Big Red Shoe with its
Big Red Heel

CLUNK!

and the other Big Red Shoe
with its Big Red Heel
CLUNK!
and before she knew it,
she was fast asleep.
And did she snore,
having danced all day
and eaten so much chicken?

YOU BET SHE DID!